UNICORN ACADEMY

The rumbling became a roar. Aisha
stared in disbelief as the top of the
mountain seemed to slide closer.
Blinking, she realized a gigantic wall
of snow was falling from the top,
straight toward them. "Avalanche!"
she shrieked.

★ ★ ★

LOOK OUT FOR MORE ADVENTURES WITH

Lily and Feather

Phoebe and Shimmer

Zara and Moonbeam

Aisha and Silver

UNICORN ACADEMY
NATURE MAGIC 4

Aisha
and
Silver

JULIE SYKES
illustrated by LUCY TRUMAN

A STEPPING STONE BOOK™
Random House New York

Text copyright © 2021 by Julie Sykes and Linda Chapman
Cover art and interior illustrations copyright © 2021 by Lucy Truman

All rights reserved. Published in the United States by Random House Children's Books, a division of Penguin Random House LLC, New York. Originally published in paperback in the United Kingdom by Nosy Crow Ltd, London, in 2021.

Random House and the colophon are registered trademarks and A Stepping Stone Book and the colophon are trademarks of Penguin Random House LLC.

Visit us on the Web! rhcbooks.com

Educators and librarians, for a variety of teaching tools, visit us at RHTeachersLibrarians.com

Library of Congress Cataloging-in-Publication Data is available upon request.
ISBN 978-0-593-42678-4 (trade) — ISBN 978-0-593-42680-7 (ebook)

Printed in the United States of America
10 9 8 7 6 5 4 3 2 1
First American Edition

To all the friends of Unicorn Academy
and to unicorn lovers everywhere

CHAPTER 1

Hail battered the roof, but Aisha ignored it. She and her unicorn, Silver, were safe and warm inside the stables at Unicorn Academy. Aisha's fingers moved quickly along her flute, playing the lively piece of music she was composing for her dorm's graduation display ride. Silver tapped along with his hooves.

Aisha had almost reached the end of the piece when Lily came into Silver's stall. Aisha paused, suddenly realizing that the hailstorm had stopped and it was quiet.

"There you are! I ran over as soon as the storm ended to check you are okay," said Lily. "The hail was huge. It did a lot of damage." Lily tucked her short dark hair behind her ears. "Trees have lost branches, and the greenhouse has been smashed." She shivered. "That's the second hailstorm in two days. It's really worrying. Zara wants us to have an Amethyst dorm meeting with our unicorns to talk about what Ms. Nettles said. Are you coming?"

Aisha remembered Ms. Nettles, the head teacher, giving a long speech that morning, but she'd been thinking about her music and had drifted off into her own thoughts. After, she'd hurried to the stables to play her piece to Silver. She frowned. "I'm working on my music."

"Please, Aisha. This is important." Lily smiled hopefully. "And we're going to play lacrosse afterward. It's much more fun with four of us."

"Let's go, Aisha," pleaded Silver. "I love lacrosse!"

Aisha shook her head. Her friends were great, but when she composed music, she couldn't relax until she was happy with it. It was like having an itch she had to scratch. "Sorry," she said. "You can tell me what you talked about later." She lifted her flute to her lips.

"Okay," said Lily, walking away. "But Zara won't be happy about this."

Aisha continued playing her music while Silver munched on his hay, until the stall door swung open. Aisha blinked in surprise when she saw Zara, Phoebe, and Lily all standing there. Zara's hands were on her hips. "Aisha," she said sternly. "Lily said you're too busy to come to our dorm meeting."

Behind Zara, Lily gave Aisha an apologetic look and shrugged.

"I'm working on my music," said Aisha. She put her flute down and tightened her high ponytail.

"Aren't you worried about what Ms. Nettles said?" Zara asked.

"It's awful!" exclaimed Phoebe. "Please come with us to talk about it, pleeeeeease!"

Aisha felt her lips twitch. Phoebe was always so dramatic.

"We're not leaving without you," Zara told her.

Aisha grinned. She knew when she wouldn't win. "All right," she said, putting her flute in its case. "I'll come."

"Yay!" Silver whinnied in delight. "We can play lacrosse!" He eagerly trotted over to the other unicorns.

"So, what did you think about what Ms. Nettles said?" Zara asked Aisha as they followed Silver. "It's really worrying, isn't it?"

"Um . . ."

Zara frowned. "Honestly, Aisha! You didn't listen! If the hailstorms get worse, then school may have to close."

"Ms. Nettles said one of us might be *killed* if we

got caught outside in a hailstorm!" Phoebe's blue eyes widened.

"She didn't exactly say that, Phoebe," said Zara carefully. "She said that if these storms continue, it will be too dangerous for us to stay at school. Graduation will have to happen early. We'd all be going home in just five days."

"That's terrible!" Aisha hated the idea of saying goodbye to her friends early. She and Silver weren't ready to graduate; he hadn't discovered his magic and they still hadn't bonded. When unicorns and their partners bonded, a strand of the person's hair turned the same color as their unicorn's mane. Then everyone could see that they were partners—and best friends—for life. If the school year ended in five days, she and Silver might not graduate and would have to return for a second year. Much as she loved Unicorn

Academy, Aisha didn't want to stay there without her roommates.

"We need to find out who's causing these hailstorms and stop them!" declared Phoebe.

Aisha's eyes widened. "You mean the hailstorms might be caused by magic?"

"Shh!" Zara said hastily, glancing around. "Let's go to the meadow where we can continue our meeting without being overheard!"

CHAPTER 2

Zara hopped onto her unicorn, Moonbeam. The others followed her lead, and soon they were all cantering out of the stable yard and past Sparkle Lake. The fountain in the middle of the lake brought magical water up from the center of the earth that then flowed all around Unicorn Island. The water made the crops and animals on the island healthy, and when the unicorns drank it, their powers were strengthened. When students of the academy graduated, they became guardians of the island and helped protect its magical waters. Aisha planned to be a composer

or a musician, but she loved knowing that she and Silver would also work together, protecting their beautiful island.

Near the meadows, the girls passed their Riding teacher, Ms. Tulip. She was walking to the stables with Mr. Long, a school inspector. He was a tall, thin man with a pointed nose and sharp eyes. He always talked as though he knew everything. Aisha felt sorry for Ms. Tulip, having to listen to him ramble on as they walked. Poor Ms. Tulip!

"Let's stay away from Mr. Long," muttered Phoebe. "He'll only ask where we're going!"

"I don't trust him at all," said Zara darkly.

Keeping their distance from Mr. Long and Ms. Tulip, they cantered into the meadow. They dismounted next to a sparkling stream and sat down on some nearby tree stumps. The unicorns splashed into the icy water, whinnying and kicking it at each other. Silver loved to play,

and he stamped his hooves harder than anyone, laughing when he soaked the others. Aisha grinned. She loved Silver so much. He was so confident and cheerful.

"All right, Amethyst dorm, down to business!" said Zara, pulling a pen and notebook out of

her pocket. "I think someone is making these hailstorms happen. My guess is that it's the same mystery person who's caused all the other problems this year—the tornadoes, the tidal wave, and the drought. If we want Unicorn Academy to stay open, we need to figure out who is responsible and stop them." She opened her notebook. "Let's go over what we know."

"The person doing these things is a man," Lily said. "We've heard him speak every time there's been a weather disaster."

"You cannot stop me," said Phoebe, making her voice sound deep and spooky, just like the voice they had heard after the weather disasters.

Aisha grinned. "That's a perfect impression, Phoebe!"

Phoebe looked pleased. She loved to act.

"Moonbeam has also seen visions of a man," said Zara. Moonbeam, her unicorn, had magic

that gave her glimpses of the future and helped her predict danger. "He's tall and skinny and wears a cloak. Because of the types of disasters, we can also guess that our suspect is someone who knows a lot about the weather."

"Mr. Long!" said Lily. "He's tall and thin, and he studied weather and geology before he became an inspector. He's also been sneaking around the school using secret tunnels!"

"And he was with us when the tidal wave hit the coast," said Phoebe. "Remember how he insisted we go camping at that exact spot! He dragged us into danger!"

"Also, we found a book in his tent with notes about how to cause purple tornadoes, volcanic eruptions, and droughts," said Zara. "That's real evidence!"

Aisha frowned. "But when we showed the notebook to Ms. Nettles, she told us that it wasn't

Mr. Long's handwriting and that the initials inside it were L.T. Mr. Long's first name is Ivor. His initials are I.L. I don't think he wrote the notes in that book, but it is odd he had it in his tent."

"The man's voice didn't sound anything like Mr. Long's, either," said Phoebe. "It was much deeper."

Zara tapped her pen against her mouth. "Okay, how about this theory? What if Mr. Long is working with the L.T. who wrote the notes in that book?"

"L.T.!" shrieked Phoebe, leaping to her feet. "Ms. Tulip's name is Larissa, so her initials are L.T.! She and Mr. Long are always hanging out. Maybe they're working together!"

"Phoebe, no! Ms. Tulip

13

is lovely. She wouldn't want to hurt the island or the unicorns," protested Lily.

"The voice in the storm definitely wasn't Ms. Tulip's," Aisha added.

Phoebe huffed. "Oh, this is all so confusing. It's making my head hurt."

Zara frowned. "The main thing is that we suspect Mr. Long is involved somehow. He may very well be working with someone. I think we should spy on him. Agreed?"

"Agreed!" everyone cried.

Zara shut her notebook with a snap. "Good. I declare this meeting closed. Now lacrosse time!"

They jumped up. The lacrosse field was next to the meadow. While the other girls gathered the unicorns, Phoebe ran to the little hut beside the playing field and took out lacrosse sticks—wooden poles with nets at the top—and the lacrosse ball.

Soon the four friends and their unicorns were

racing up and down the field. Zara and Phoebe were on one team, and Lily and Aisha were on the other. There were two goals, one at each end of the field. The ball had to be thrown from person to person using the sticks. When a team threw it into their goal, they scored a point. Magic wasn't allowed, but everyone knew it was more fun if that rule was broken.

"Yay!" Phoebe caught the ball, but just as she aimed for the goal, it rose out of her net and floated away. "Hey!" she yelled.

Lily, giggling, held out her net as Feather brought the ball to them using her moving magic. Seconds before it reached Lily, Zara and Moonbeam galloped in front of them.

Zara swung her stick and snatched the ball from the air.

"Faster!" Zara urged as Moonbeam raced toward the goal. She hurled the ball forward, and it flew through the goal. "Yay!"

"How did you do that?" spluttered Lily.

Zara grinned. "Moonbeam used her magic to see what you were going to do, so we stopped you!"

Lily scooped the ball up with her net and rode to the center to continue the game. She threw it to Aisha, who caught it. Silver charged toward their goal, but as Aisha threw it at the goal, the ball seemed to hit something invisible. Rebounding, it flew straight down the field and into Phoebe's waiting net. Phoebe threw it into her and Zara's goal. "Two–zero!" she whooped. Getting a strong whiff of burnt sugar, Aisha knew Shimmer had used his magic—he could make balls of energy.

"It's not fair!" said Silver. "I wish I had magic."

"We'll find out what your magic is soon," Aisha said.

Silver's ears pricked. "You're right," he said. "I bet I'll discover my powers any day now!"

They kept playing, but as Lily scored, Aisha noticed something. "It's getting really dark."

They all looked up. The sun had disappeared behind heavy black clouds.

Zara looked alarmed. "Those look like hail clouds. We'd better get inside!"

They put the equipment away and set off across the meadow at a gallop. They were only just in time. As they dived into the stables, huge hail started to fall. They watched from the doorway as the hail dropped like stones and splintered into icy shards on the ground.

"Thank goodness we're not out in that," said Lily.

"That is definitely not normal hail," said Zara grimly. "If this is Mr. Long's fault, we have to stop him!"

Behind them, a man snapped, "If what is my fault?" They swung around. Mr. Long was coming out of the tack room with Ms. Tulip.

"Nothing!" Zara said quickly.

Mr. Long looked at them suspiciously.

"Come on now, girls," said Ms. Tulip. "There's no point hanging around at the doorway. Lead your unicorns to their stalls, and then sweep the aisles for me."

The girls sighed and set to work.

As Zara led Moonbeam into the stall next to Silver's, she whispered to Aisha, "I bet he *is* responsible, you know."

Moonbeam's eyes took on a faraway look. She swayed and spoke dreamily. *"Danger comes from the frozen heights. . . . He watches. . . . Revenge is in his heart."*

She blinked. "Oh, I just had one of my visions."

Zara and Aisha exchanged looks. "You said danger was coming, and a man who wanted revenge was watching," said Aisha.

Moonbeam shivered. "Yes, I saw a man watching us through a telescope. A tall, thin man."

"Mr. Long?" asked Zara eagerly.

"I'm . . . I'm not sure," Moonbeam hesitated. "I couldn't see his face. It might have been him."

Zara lifted her chin. "Well, if he's watching us, we're going to watch him back!" she declared. "We're going to solve this mystery once and for all!"

CHAPTER 3

Dinner that night was steaming bowls of stew with crusty bread, followed by delicious chocolate pudding. Aisha was scraping up the last spoonful of pudding when Ms. Nettles stood up and clapped her hands for silence.

"I'm afraid I have some very bad news. The two hailstorms today smashed most of the equipment on the playground, along with several windows in the school building. The teachers and I have decided that for everyone's safety, Unicorn Academy must close early." Ms. Nettles paused as a huge groan went up from the room. "The graduation ceremony will be earlier. It will now be in five days."

"Five days!" whispered Aisha.

"That's not much time to find Silver's magic," said Lily anxiously.

Aisha bit her lip.

"We will let your parents know," Ms. Nettles continued. "Please also check the weather carefully every time you go outside. Luckily, no one was hurt today. If the sky looks threatening, stay indoors. If you do get caught in a hailstorm, then find somewhere safe to take shelter. Do not try to make it back to the academy until the storm has passed."

As she walked from the hall with the other teachers, the students erupted in noisy chatter.

"What am I going to do?" said Aisha. "Five days isn't long enough to find Silver's magic and

bond with him, and I have to complete the music for our display ride."

"The music is great. Just concentrate on you and Silver," said Lily.

Aisha felt torn. She wanted to find Silver's magic and bond with him, but she wanted her music for the display ride to be perfect. Then, if she and Silver didn't get to graduate, at least the others would have wonderful music when they performed for their parents.

"Five days isn't enough time to do anything!" exclaimed Phoebe.

"We need to solve the mystery behind the hailstorms," said Zara. "If we do that, we'll still have a whole month here. Let's follow Mr. Long!"

They quickly cleared their plates and left. Mr. Long and Ms. Tulip were talking quietly farther down the hall. Zara nodded toward the statue of a unicorn, and the four of them ducked behind

it. When Mr. Long and Ms. Tulip headed for the staff cloakroom, the girls followed, hiding in an empty classroom as Mr. Long and Ms. Tulip paused to put on coats and boots.

"Why are they always together?" whispered Lily.

"I still think she might be working with him!" Phoebe hissed back.

Zara made frantic *shh*-ing gestures as Mr. Long glanced in their direction. He looked around for a moment, then said something to Ms. Tulip, and the two of them went out into the frosty night.

The girls tiptoed after them across the grass. Mr. Long and Ms. Tulip seemed to be heading for the stables. They were talking, but their voices were so quiet that the girls couldn't catch what they were saying. Aisha felt a flicker of suspicion. What were they whispering to each other? Could Phoebe be right about Ms. Tulip?

Suddenly Phoebe stepped on a frozen puddle and slipped. She shrieked as she fell. Mr. Long and Ms. Tulip swung around.

"What are you all doing?" demanded Mr. Long, striding over.

"I expect the girls are here to settle their unicorns, Ivor, like they do every night," said Ms. Tulip.

"Yes, that's right!" said Zara quickly. "We're here for our unicorns."

"Hmm." Mr. Long gave them a suspicious look.

"Are you okay, Phoebe?" Ms. Tulip asked as Lily and Aisha helped her up.

"I'm fine," said Phoebe.

"Good. Let's hurry inside, out of the cold," said Ms. Tulip.

"Mr. Long, why are you here?" Zara asked as they all entered the stables. "You don't have a unicorn."

The top of Mr. Long's cheeks flushed red. "I'm . . . Um . . ."

"Mr. Long kindly offered to help me with my evening stable rounds," Ms. Tulip said. "Now come

along, girls. It's getting late." She hurried away to the feed room with Mr. Long following her.

"Suspicious behavior," Zara whispered to the others. "Very suspicious."

Some more students arrived, and under the watchful eye of Ms. Tulip, everyone made sure their unicorns had fluffy straw beds, full hay nets, and clean water.

Silver nuzzled Aisha as she tied up his hay net. "Maybe tomorrow we could see if we can find my magic," he said hopefully. "I think I'm very close to discovering it. I stamped my hoof earlier, and I'm sure I saw a faint pink spark. Feather told me that's one of the first signs."

"Mmm," said Aisha, not really listening. She was watching Zara and Moonbeam in the next stall. Moonbeam's eyes were half shut, and she was swaying from side to side.

Silver stamped a hoof. "Aisha, I'm beginning to think you don't care if I find my—"

"Shh," Aisha interrupted, nodding at Moonbeam.

Moonbeam's eyelids were fluttering. *"The tall figure watches with his telescope. Look to the north. Silver . . . NO!"*

Moonbeam's eyes snapped open in alarm. Aisha and Silver hurried to the partition.

"Was that another vision, Moonbeam?" asked Silver.

Moonbeam nodded. "I saw the cloaked man with a telescope again. I saw you too, Silver, but then you just vanished." She looked worried. "I had a real feeling of danger!"

Silver gulped. "Oh."

"How did he vanish?" asked Zara curiously.

"He just disappeared!" said Moonbeam.

"But where did I go?" Silver said, his voice

trembling slightly. For once his confidence seemed to have left him.

"I don't know," said Moonbeam. "Sorry."

Ms. Tulip came down the walkway between the stalls, whistling. The tune made an idea jump into Aisha's head for her piece of music for the display ride. It was happy and fun, just what she needed. She hummed her idea to herself. Yes—it was perfect!

"Are you done, girls?" Ms. Tulip said. "If so, you should be getting back to your dorm."

Aisha's fingers were itching to try the tune out on her flute. "I'm finished, Ms. Tulip." She quickly kissed Silver's cheek. "Night, Silver."

"Wait, Aisha!" Silver pawed the ground. "We need to talk about Moonbeam's vision. What if I do just disappear?"

Aisha frowned. It wasn't like Silver to worry about things. She hesitated. She really wanted

to go work on her music. Silver would cheer up soon, she was sure of it. "We can talk tomorrow. Don't worry about it now."

"But—" Silver began.

Aisha didn't stop. "Night, Silver!" she called.

She hurried out of the stall, her mind filled with the melody she wanted to add to her composition. She ran straight back to the dorm, humming to herself as she went.

CHAPTER 4

The next morning, the first lesson was geography with Ms. Rivers. "Today we are going to learn about tornadoes," she told the class. "Mr. Long is an expert on weather conditions and has offered to show us an experiment. He's waiting for us outside."

They followed Ms. Rivers out to the stable yard. Zara nudged Aisha. "An expert on weather conditions," she muttered darkly. "Do you think that includes using weather to damage the island? I wonder what he knows about hailstorms!"

Aisha had to admit that it seemed suspicious.

As the class gathered around him, Mr. Long clapped his hands together. "Today we shall look at tornadoes and the effects of combining magic and science. As I hope you know by now, some magic and scientific reactions are reversible, but not when the magic and science are combined."

Aisha started to think about her piece of music as Mr. Long kept talking. She couldn't wait to play it to Silver. Zara nudged her, and she realized everyone was following Mr. Long to a nearby water trough.

"First, I'm going to demonstrate how we can create a mini tornado in this bottle using science." He picked up a large glass jar with a lid from beside the trough. It was filled with water.

"Watch carefully, please." Mr. Long unscrewed the lid and added a few drops of green liquid.

"What's that, sir? Is it a magic potion?" asked Spike from Topaz dorm.

"No," said Mr. Long in his usual clipped tone. "It's a simple detergent. The sparkly powder I'm adding now is purple glitter to help you see the tornado." He screwed the lid on to the jar tightly, and, turning it upside down, he spun it in a circular motion before holding it still. "Observe, a mini tornado in a jar." He brought it closer so they could all see.

"Look, Aisha," said Zara, nudging her.

Aisha stared at the tiny glittering tornado whirling in the water, momentarily distracted from her music. "That's so cool!"

Mr. Long looked pleased at the response. "Spinning the jar created a water vortex that

looks like a mini tornado. Science is a wonderful thing. When scientific knowledge is combined with magic, the possibilities are endless!" His eyes lost their usual disapproving expression, and his face lit up.

"What do you mean, sir?" asked Johan, Spike's friend.

"We can use science to strengthen magic, or magic to strengthen science, making the effects bigger!" Mr. Long said enthusiastically. "When I was a researcher, I worked alongside the genius Count Lysander Thornberry."

"Not him again," muttered Phoebe. Mr. Long was always talking about the count. He was a scientist and inventor who lived as a hermit.

"The rain machine he made was a major breakthrough in using science to strengthen magic," Mr. Long went on. "The count took rain seeds, which are magic seeds from the ocean

that can make it rain. He used them to create a machine that strengthened the seeds so that more rain fell, and also allowed the count to make it rain wherever he wanted. It was amazing." He sighed. "The count could have achieved so much if he hadn't shut himself away in his castle." He shook his head. "A brilliant but flawed man."

Zara put up her hand. "Sir, are you going to combine magic and science today?"

"I am," Mr. Long said. "Phoebe, will you please get Shimmer from the stables?"

Looking surprised, Phoebe went to get her unicorn. Mr. Long spoke to Shimmer. "I need your help, Shimmer. Will you please use your magic when I ask?" Shimmer nodded and blew his long pink-and-blue forelock out of his eyes.

"Everyone, observe the mini tornado." Mr. Long spun the jar again, then held it up for

everyone to see. The water tornado twirled gently. "Now, Shimmer, please use your energy magic to make the tornado spin faster. Just a little bit will work."

Shimmer stamped his hoof. A ball of energy shot into the air and hit the jar. The bottled tornado immediately grew bigger and spun faster. "See!" cried Mr. Long, as the jar shook in his hands. "Keep back!" he ordered. He put the jar down and backed away.

"Again, please, Shimmer!" he called as the jar rattled.

Shimmer stamped his hoof. A larger ball of energy hit the jar.

There was a sharp crack and the jar's lid flew across the yard. Everyone gasped as whirling water shot high up, drawing in water from the nearby trough, before suddenly bursting into a

cloud of sparkling raindrops that soaked them all.

"Behold the power of magic and science!" Mr. Long bowed and held out his hand, motioning for Shimmer to bow too. The class whooped and cheered. Mr. Long beamed, looking nothing like his usual stern self.

"Putting science and magic together is amazing, sir!" said Spike.

"I want to try!" said Phoebe.

Mr. Long's eyes gleamed. "There is no limit to the amazing things that can be done when a unicorn with Shimmer's power combines his magic with science."

Even strict Ms. Rivers looked impressed. "That was wonderful. Thank you very much, Mr. Long," she said warmly. "Inside, everyone, and I'll give you some homework!"

When Ms. Rivers dismissed them for lunch, Aisha didn't go with the others to get something to eat. Instead, she hurried back to the stables to see Silver.

"I made some changes to my music last night. Can I play it for you?" Aisha was already pulling

her flute from its case. She blew softly into it, closing her eyes as the music took her over. When she'd finished, she smiled to herself. "What do you think?"

Silver rubbed his head on her arm. "It's great."

"Really?" Aisha's chest swelled with pride. "You're not just saying that? Which part did you like best?"

"All of it. It's perfect," said Silver.

"But . . . ?" asked Aisha, sensing there was more.

Silver let out a long breath. "I can't stop thinking about what Moonbeam said about me vanishing. It scared me. You said we could talk about it today."

Aisha tried to hide her disappointment. She'd thought Silver was going to say something more about her music. "I really wouldn't worry about it. Moonbeam's visions are hard to understand. I'm sure you're not actually going to disappear."

"But what if I do?" said Silver doubtfully. "What if I'm kidnapped or something?"

"Aisha!" The rest of Amethyst dorm called her.

Aisha went to the stables' doors. "I'm here. What's up?" she said, seeing their excited faces as they came up to the Amethyst dorm stables.

"Ms. Nettles just made an announcement," said Zara. "Because of graduation being early, lessons have been canceled so people can practice for the display ride. Then tomorrow there's a picnic ride to the ruined tower."

"Or students can spend time with their unicorns, trying to bond and find their magic," said Lily.

"I know," said Phoebe suddenly. "Ms. Rosemary said she got some new hair crayons that we can use to decorate our unicorns for the display. They're like hair dye, but better because they wash out. Let's ask if we can practice with them. It'll give

you and Silver some time together to try to find his magic."

"Oooh, yes," said Silver, tossing his mane. "I'd like that."

"Sounds good to me!" said Zara.

"Okay," sighed Aisha. She could tell from Silver's hopeful look that he liked the idea of having a pamper session and going on the picnic ride.

"I'll go ask Ms. Rosemary where the crayons are," said Phoebe.

Five minutes later, she came back with a big box full of hair crayons and glittery hoof polish in different colors. "You just rub the crayons on the mane or tail, and then the color sets after half an hour. They'll wash out with hot water. It sounds simple enough! I'm going to turn Shimmer's mane and tail gold!"

They all got together and started decorating
their unicorns. Aisha painted pink glitter on
Silver's hooves and colored his mane and tail.
"You look just like Shimmer!" She giggled as she
changed his green-silver-red mane and tail to
pink and pale blue.

Silver tossed his mane in delight. "I like it. It's

fun to look different!" He nuzzled her. "I can't wait until we bond and you get a green-silver-red streak in your hair to match my real mane and tail colors."

Aisha smiled. "Me too."

After their pamper session, the girls and their unicorns went for a ride on the academy grounds. Aisha and Silver had fun, even though Silver didn't seem any closer to discovering his magic. In the afternoon, the dorm decided to spy on Mr. Long in the stables.

"What's he doing now?" hissed Zara as they peered out from behind a stack of hay bales.

"Counting buckets," Aisha said.

"I can see that, but why?" said Zara.

"Maybe he likes buckets?" suggested Phoebe.

Lily snorted with laughter. Mr. Long turned

around. They all ducked back behind the bales.

"It's okay, he's not coming over," whispered Zara, peeking out.

Mr. Long tucked his clipboard under his arm and walked slowly down the aisle.

"He's going into that empty stall," Zara whispered. They tiptoed after him and were almost at the door when Mr. Long came back out.

"I knew it!" he cried. "I thought I was being spied upon! Zara, Phoebe, and Lily—you will come with me to Ms. Nettles's office right now. Unicorns, back to your stalls immediately!"

He led Zara, Phoebe, and Lily toward the exit but completely ignored Aisha.

Aisha stared at Silver in confusion. "What's going on? Why did he leave me behind?" she whispered as Mr. Long marched the others away.

Silver looked puzzled "I don't know."

"I'd better go with them," said Aisha.

She hugged Silver and ran after the others. She wasn't going to let them take all the blame when she'd been there too.

"Where did you and Silver go?" Zara whispered, looking impressed. "Next time, I'm hiding with you!"

Aisha was confused. "What do you mean? We weren't hiding."

"Silence!" snapped Mr. Long. "No talking! Ms. Nettles will deal with you!"

Ms. Nettles was very upset when Mr. Long told her what had happened. "Girls," she said after he had left. "I am very disappointed in you. After the summer drought, I thought I made it quite clear that Mr. Long is not causing these events and has nothing to do with them. I also made it clear that you were to leave any investigating to me. I will *not* have you spying on Mr. Long in this way. He has the very best interests of both the academy and Unicorn Island at heart. Please leave the inspector alone, or there will be serious consequences. Do I make myself clear?"

"Yes, Ms. Nettles," the girls said sheepishly.

"As punishment, you will have detention in the library tomorrow with Mr. Long supervising," said Ms. Nettles.

"But everyone else is going on the picnic ride!" said Zara.

"Well, maybe you should have thought of that before you spied on Mr. Long," said Ms. Nettles. "Detention tomorrow, girls, and that's that!"

CHAPTER 5

Phoebe groaned as she looked through a big pile of books in the library the next morning. "I wish we were out riding instead of being cooped up here."

"Me too," sighed Aisha. She wished she were playing her flute instead of writing reports on extreme weather for Mr. Long. He would be back in a few hours and expected the work to be done by then.

"There's nothing about magic hailstorms in these books," said Lily. "I thought this detention might be a good chance to try to find out more, but all the hailstorms I've read about are normal ones."

"This is interesting," said Zara, holding up a thick leather book. "It's about avalanches."

"So is this," said Aisha. "It's all about the Frozen Wastelands, where there are dangerous things like avalanches and saber-toothed polar bears. There's also a glacier that has special pink diamonds trapped under the ice. If you find one, you can use it to undo any freezing spell. It sounds like an amazing place."

"This one mentions the Frozen Wastelands too," said Lily, holding up a very old, thin book. "It was tucked behind another book at the back of the bookshelf. It's a biography about Count Thornberry. It says he has a lab hidden in the ice caves of Diamond Glacier."

"He's the person Mr. Long is always talking about, isn't he?" said Aisha.

"I thought he lived in the south of the island," said Zara.

"His family castle is there, but his lab is in the Frozen Wastelands according to this," said Lily. "It says he's worked in secret since he left the university."

She read from the book: *"The count was furious when leading scientists questioned his methods, worried that he could damage the natural world by using magic to strengthen science. Angered by this, the count hid away and refused to share his work with the rest of the scientific community."* Lily turned the page. "There's a picture of him here. Look at that mustache!" She turned the book around to show everyone.

Phoebe squealed. "Oh my gosh!"

"What?" demanded Zara.

"Look at him!" said Phoebe, jabbing her finger at the picture.

"He's tall and thin and wearing a cloak. Could he be the man Moonbeam sees in her visions?" She ticked things off on her fingers. "He's smart. He's angry with people on the island, which could mean he wants revenge. He knows about weather. . . ."

Zara pointed at the picture. "And look at this design on the pocket of his cloak." She gasped. "It's just like the one on the button we found in that ruined cottage, near where the tidal wave hit!"

"Lysander Thornberry," said Lily quickly. "L.T. Those were the initials in the notebook about weather disasters that we found in Mr. Long's tent!"

"You know what this means?" exclaimed Phoebe. "Drum roll, please!" She drummed her hands on the desk. "I bet that we just found out who Mr. Long is working with!"

Aisha stiffened. A drum roll would be perfect for the climax of her piece of music. She tried to fit one into the music in her head. Yes! It was the final thing she needed! She was so excited, she barely heard the rest of her friends' conversation.

"It's a good theory, Phoebe," said Zara, "but we need actual evidence before we go to Ms. Nettles. She's upset enough as it is. I vote when we write our reports, we don't put in any of this stuff about Count Thornberry. We don't want to make Mr. Long think we're on to him. Let's keep this between ourselves for now, agreed?"

"Agreed," said Lily and Phoebe.

"Aisha?" said Zara. "Do you agree?"

"Yes, of course," said Aisha, busy thinking about drum rolls.

Zara smiled. "Great. Let's write our reports so we can be free from detention!"

Everyone began to write. But Aisha started

humming again and tapping her fingers on the desk.

"Aisha! Write!" Zara ordered, handing her a pen. "Unless you want to stay in here all day!"

Aisha definitely didn't want to do that! Grabbing the nearest book, she started to write her report.

When Mr. Long returned, he took their work with a sniff. Whooping for joy, the girls raced outside to the stables. On the way to Silver's stall, Aisha grabbed a handful of sky berries for him, stuffing them in her pocket as a treat for later.

"Silver! I think I've finally finished the music! Will you listen to it? We can go in the barn—it'll be quieter there."

They went into the barn next door to the stables. Aisha shut the door behind them, and they settled behind the piled-up bales of hay.

"I can finally play you the whole piece now," said Aisha, feeding him some of the berries.

"All right," said Silver, gobbling them up. "But then I want to talk to you. Moonbeam had another vision. She said she saw me vanish again."

"Mmm," said Aisha, only half listening as she got her flute out of its case.

"Please, Aisha. I really do want to talk about this. I'm worried," said Silver. "There was a plan to kidnap unicorns a year ago and—" He broke off as they heard adult voices outside the barn door. "It's Mr. Long and Ms. Tulip!"

"Shh," said Aisha. "They're probably just getting a bale of hay." She stroked Silver's mane as the door creaked open.

Mr. Long and Ms. Tulip came in and shut the door behind them.

Ms. Tulip giggled. "Why are we here, Ivor?"

"I needed to talk to you in private," said Mr. Long. "This is very important."

Aisha stiffened. What was Mr. Long about to say? She leaned forward to listen, her heart pounding. But as she did so, she dropped her flute, and it clattered to the ground.

Aisha quickly grabbed it. She and Silver looked at each other, horrified.

"What was that?" Mr. Long snapped.

"I don't know," said Ms. Tulip.

"What should we do?" Aisha mouthed to Silver.

Silver looked around desperately, but there was nowhere they could hide. A smell of burnt sugar wafted through the air.

"The noise came from over there!" Mr. Long said. Footsteps thumped across the barn.

Aisha froze. She and Silver were about to be discovered! She hugged Silver's neck and buried her face in his thick mane as Mr. Long peered around the hay bales. . . .

CHAPTER 6

Aisha expected to hear Mr. Long shout her name. But to her surprise, she heard him say, "There's nothing here, Larissa."

She looked up from Silver's mane. Mr. Long was looking straight at her, but he turned back to Ms. Tulip. "I don't know what caused that noise, but there's no one here. Now, Larissa . . ." Mr. Long took several deep breaths. "I am so happy that I came to inspect Unicorn Academy because it led to meeting you." Aisha peeked out from behind the bales and saw him blush. "Yes, you, Larissa Tulip. You fill me with more joy than you

could ever imagine. I love you." He cleared his throat. "Dare I . . . Might I . . . Is it possible to believe you feel the same?"

"Oh, Ivor! Yes! Yes, I do!" cried Ms. Tulip. She hurried over to him and took his hands. "I love you, Ivor Long!"

They beamed at each other and then . . . they kissed!

Aisha's mouth fell open. Mr. Long and Ms. Tulip were *in love*?

Mr. Long pushed a strand of hair behind Ms. Tulip's ear and offered her his hand. Smiling at him, she took it and they walked out of the barn.

"Oh. My. Goodness!" Aisha breathed slowly. "I really wish I could unsee that."

Silver looked just as shocked as she felt. "Totally!" He shut his eyes and shook his head. "They're in *lurve*!"

"I can't believe it! And why did Mr. Long keep talking to Ms. Tulip when he knew we were here behind the bales?" Aisha said. "We need to talk to the others about this!"

They were hurrying across the barn when the door opened and the rest of Amethyst dorm and their unicorns looked in.

"There you are!" cried Zara. "We've been searching for you everywhere. What are you doing in here?"

"That doesn't matter," said Aisha. "Just wait until you hear what we just saw!"

"Mr. Long loves Ms. Tulip!" exclaimed Silver.

"No!" squealed Phoebe.

"Yes!" Aisha quickly explained.

"That's so weird," said Phoebe. "Ms. Tulip's lovely. She's far too nice for Mr. Long."

Lily frowned. "What I don't understand is why he didn't get upset with Aisha and Silver for

spying on him. And why didn't he tell them to get out of the barn?"

"I have no idea," said Aisha. "He just seemed to look right through us—it was like we were invisible."

Phoebe turned to Aisha. "That's it! Silver has invisibility magic! There's a boy in my drama club at home whose unicorn has invisibility magic— it's so awesome."

"It would explain why I keep seeing Silver vanish!" said Moonbeam.

"But Silver didn't vanish, I could see him the whole time," argued Aisha. "And even if Silver could turn invisible, wouldn't Mr. Long have still seen me?"

"Not if you were touching Silver!" exclaimed Phoebe. "If a unicorn has invisibility magic and their partner is touching their mane, then they also turn invisible."

Silver gave Aisha an excited look. "I felt a tingling in my hooves just before Mr. Long looked around the bales. I really wanted to help you hide. I was so worried you were going to get into trouble. Maybe I do have invisibility magic."

"Invisibility magic would explain why Mr. Long didn't see either of you when he caught us spying on him the other day," said Lily.

"Try it now," said Zara.

Silver took a breath and stamped a hoof on the ground. A sugary smell filled the air, and pink sparks swirled around his and Aisha's legs. His eyes widened, and Aisha gasped.

"Wow!" breathed Zara. "Your legs vanished!"

Silver stamped again, and Aisha saw her friends' eyes go big.

"They're gone!" cried Lily.

"We can't see you at all!" said Zara. "Are you still there?"

Aisha grinned and gently tugged Silver's mane, moving her head. He nodded, understanding what she wanted to do. They tiptoed behind Zara. "BOO!" Aisha exclaimed.

Zara shrieked and jumped. Silver stamped his hoof again.

"We can see you now!" cried Phoebe as Silver and Aisha burst out laughing.

Zara joined in. "Invisibility magic is totally awesome!" She high-fived Aisha.

"You know what this means?" said Lily in delight. "You just need to bond, and then you can graduate."

"Hooray!" Silver whinnied. He broke off as the barn door slammed open and an icy wind swirled inside.

"What's happening?" said Phoebe as the wind started spinning and moving toward them. Loose

hay and dust from the floor were pulled into it, spinning around faster and faster.

"Twisters don't just suddenly form inside a barn," said Zara uneasily. "Everyone on their unicorns, now!"

The girls climbed onto their unicorns, but the wind had already reached Silver. It encircled him and Aisha. A familiar voice echoed out. *"I've been watching you. I want you. Come!"*

"Help!" yelled Aisha as she and Silver were lifted into the air.

"Aisha!" Zara shrieked. She grabbed Aisha's coat just as Phoebe and Lily grabbed onto Silver's mane, and the cyclone whirled all of the girls and their unicorns away.

CHAPTER 7

The girls clung to each other tightly as they spun around. Suddenly they dropped and landed with a bump. The freezing air bit into Aisha's cheeks as she stared at the strange, frozen world around them.

"Where are we?" As she spoke, her breath froze in a cloud of ice crystals. She spotted a glint of something pink near her feet. She picked it up. "A pink diamond! I read about them in detention. They can melt anything. They're only found on Diamond Glacier in the Frozen Wastelands!"

The glacier was covered by a thin layer of snow. Underneath, thick ice glistened. They were a little below the peak of a huge mountain. Mist swirled over the glacier, and snow-covered cliffs rose up on either side of them.

"But why are we here? And what was that twister? Where did it come from? Ouch!" cried Lily as a ball of ice fell from the sky and hit her arm. Another fell, and then another. Dark clouds were gathering overhead.

"It's a hailstorm!" whinnied Silver.

"Quick, over there!" Zara shouted. She pointed to a dark opening in the mountain.

They scrambled across the glacier. Once everyone was safely inside the large cave, the girls dismounted. Aisha shivered. The walls were crusted over with ice. Pointed, white icicles hung from the ceiling like jagged teeth. At the back of

the cave, a tunnel led farther into the mountain.

"That storm is dangerous!" said Phoebe as the hail pounded down outside.

"It's not the only thing that's dangerous," said Zara worriedly. "Saber-toothed polar bears live in the Frozen Wastelands. They attack on sight." She looked around. "I hope one doesn't live in this cave."

"Why are we here?" Lily said. "Did you all hear that voice in the twister?"

Phoebe nodded and mimicked it. *"I've been watching you. I want you. Come!"*

"Someone obviously used magic to bring us here," said Zara grimly.

There was a laugh from behind them and a flash of green light. "Not just magic, but magic and science combined!" They all swung around as a tall man in a long black cloak stepped out from the back of the cave. He had a pointed mustache

and slicked-back dark hair. Silver rings glinted on his long fingers as he rubbed his hands together.

"Count Thornberry!" gasped Aisha, recognizing him from the picture in the book.

"Yes!" the count bowed. "I brought you here using a wind created by one of my weather machines."

Zara was angry. "You kidnapped us? Why?"

"Because I need one of you," the count said.

"Which one?" demanded Zara.

"The unicorn who is the energy thrower. The one with the pink-and-blue mane who destroyed my tidal wave." The count pointed at Silver, his eyes gleaming. "I have been watching you from afar using a magic telescope. If I use your power to strengthen my inventions, I will be able to bring this island to its knees!"

Aisha realized the count had made a mistake. He thought Silver was Shimmer because Silver's

mane and tail were colored pink and blue from the hair crayons. "But that's not—"

Silver cut her off. "What do you want me to do?" he asked boldly, stepping forward.

Aisha stared at him. Why was her unicorn

pretending to be Shimmer? Silver's eyes met hers briefly and he winked. She hoped that he had a plan. She felt sick at the thought of him putting himself in danger.

The count addressed Silver. "With your energy magic and my weather machines, we can create the biggest ice storm ever. The purple tornadoes, the tidal wave, the heat wave, they were just practice for the main event. This winter storm will cover Unicorn Island in a solid sheet of ice. Neither science nor magic could do something this big on its own. When we succeed, I, Count Lysander Thornberry the Eighth, will be taken seriously at last!"

The girls' shocked silence was broken by a roar. A huge saber-toothed polar bear was in the entrance to the cave. Its small eyes gleamed, and long teeth curved out of its mouth. Phoebe and

Lily screamed, and the unicorns whinnied in alarm.

The bear's tiny eyes blazed as it reared up, slashing at the air. It opened its mouth and roared again.

Quicker than lightning, the count pulled a small device from his pocket. Holding it steady, he pressed a blue button. A jet of water shot across the cave and covered the angry bear. As the water hit the bear's fur, it froze. The bear slowed and stiffened in place, becoming an ice statue.

The count smiled, but the smile did not reach his eyes. "That is just a small example of what

I can do. Come with me, energy unicorn," he ordered, pointing at the tunnel behind him.

"No," said Silver bravely. "You can't make me help you."

The count glanced at the frozen saber-toothed polar bear. Then, holding up the portable weather machine, he aimed it at Silver. "I think I can."

Silver stood his ground. "I won't be able to help you if you freeze me."

Count Thornberry moved the machine so that it pointed at the others. "That's true, but I don't need your friends. If you don't help me, you can watch them turn to ice." A twisted smile spread across his face. "One by one!"

CHAPTER 8

Count Thornberry aimed his weather machine at the group and pressed a gray button.

"No!" Shimmer whinnied in alarm.

Aisha gasped, convinced they were about to be frozen. But instead, a tornado spiraled out of the machine and swept toward them, getting bigger by the second.

"Run!" cried Zara. But before they could try to escape, the freezing wind swept them up. Aisha felt like a marble being pushed down a twisty tube. Several breathless minutes later, the wind started to slow. Aisha felt Silver nudge her

urgently. "Aisha! Hold my mane!" he whispered.

She grabbed on just as the wind died and they dropped to the ground. Aisha's legs wobbled as she clambered to her feet, still hanging on to Silver's mane. They had landed at the end of a tunnel outside a cave that had a door made of metal bars. Glowing green icicles hung from the ceiling, providing the only light. The count was facing them. Aisha smelled a whiff of burnt sugar and was sure that Silver was using his magic.

He started to back slowly away from the others. Aisha moved silently beside him. She wished she knew what he was planning, but she trusted him completely. She could feel Silver breathing heavily. Doing magic took a lot of effort when unicorns first discovered their powers. She rubbed Silver's neck, silently sending him her love and support. Silver nuzzled her gratefully.

"Get inside," said the count, waving his device.

"No, wait!" He took a step forward. "There were eight of you. Now there are only six. Where's the energy unicorn and his partner? What have you done with them?"

Aisha held her breath as she saw the others look around and realize the count was right. *Please let them figure out what we've just done,* she prayed.

Phoebe suddenly stomped forward, looking outraged. "What have *we* done with them?" she cried. "First, you kidnapped us from our school, and now you've brought us down to this dump, losing our best friend and her unicorn on the way. It's not what *we've* done with them, it's what *you've* done!"

"Your magic machine must have left them behind!" Zara shouted, joining in.

"Pah!" the count spat. "Get in that cave, and I'll go fetch them!"

They filed inside. The count slammed the metal

door shut and turned a key in the lock. Then he marched away, his black cloak rippling behind him. As his footsteps grew fainter, Silver let out a sigh.

"Phew! I wasn't going to be able to keep us invisible for much longer!" He leaned against the icy wall, panting for breath.

"You were amazing." Aisha kissed his neck. She searched in her pocket and found a few remaining sky berries from earlier. "It's not much, but these might help."

Sky berries gave unicorns strength and helped replenish their magic. Silver gobbled them up gratefully.

"Aisha! Is that you and Silver out there?" Zara hissed through the door.

"Yes! Silver used his magic to trick the count," said Aisha, hurrying to the bars.

"Ha!" said Phoebe. "The count's not as smart as he thinks!"

"Definitely not. He left the key in the door," said Aisha. The lock was stiff, and it took both hands to turn the huge key. But, finally, there was a click and the door swung open. The others raced out, except for Moonbeam, who was swaying on the spot.

"Beware the falling ceiling . . . Watch for the spears of ice. . . . Take the left turn. . . ."

There was a large grating noise. Glancing up, Aisha saw a crack run across the ceiling. "Maybe he is quite smart!" she gasped. "I think the cave might have a spell on it, and it's just noticed you've escaped!"

"Moonbeam!" cried Zara.

Moonbeam jerked out of her vision. She cantered out. Zara leaped onto her back. "Gallop!" she shrieked. "Before the roof comes down!"

The walls began to shake as the crack spread

along the ceiling of the tunnel. The unicorns ran down the icy passageway, the girls clinging on desperately as the crack snaked after them. The glowing icicles smashed down one by one as the crack passed them. The unicorns raced by a brightly lit lab in an enormous cavern. It must be where the count ran his experiments! But they couldn't stop. They had to get out! Aisha shrieked as one of the icicles fell right at Silver's hooves.

The tunnel began to widen. Aisha saw two tunnels ahead, one leading to the left and one to the right. The one to the right had extra-long icicles hanging from the ceiling, and there was a frozen bear in the entrance. "That's the way out!" she shouted. But as she spoke, Moonbeam pulled up suddenly, and the other unicorns almost crashed into her, their hooves skidding across the ice.

"Turn back! That cave was in my vision!" whinnied Moonbeam. She swung around, forcing everyone away from the tunnel. "Back! Back!"

Just as they went back, there was a huge *whump*. The icicles hanging from the ceiling of the tunnel all fell like deadly spears.

Phoebe's face was whiter than the ice. "That was close! Imagine if we'd been in there!"

"I think you just saved our lives, Moonbeam," said Feather shakily.

"We have to find another way out," said Zara.

"Moonbeam, you said *turn left* when you were having your last vision," Lily said. She pointed to the left-hand tunnel. "Let's go left."

They set off again.

"Faster, Moonbeam!" urged Zara.

They galloped along the twisty tunnel, the unicorns' hooves slipping and sliding.

"Look out!" Zara yelled over her shoulder as they approached a big crack in the ground. Moonbeam leaped into the air and cleared it.

Aisha caught her breath as Silver leaped too. For a terrifying moment, the hole stretched beneath them, a black void, but then Silver landed safely on the other side. Fresh air blasted Aisha as they followed Zara around a corner. Daylight streamed in from a wide opening. A few steps later and they were galloping out onto the glacier with its snow-covered cliffs on either side.

Phoebe whooped. "We made it! We escaped!"

Looking higher up the glacier, Aisha saw the frozen saber-toothed polar bear at the entrance to the cave. She flung her arms around Silver and hugged him tight. "Silver, you're amazing! I was terrified when you said you were Shimmer. But you were so brave. Your idea of turning invisible to help everyone escape was genius, and"—a

shudder ran through her—"I was so scared, I thought the count was going to do something horrible to you."

Silver nuzzled her. "I felt the same when I thought he might turn you into ice. I don't know what I'd do if something happened to you."

Aisha buried her face in his mane. Suddenly she realized that though her music was important, nothing in the world mattered as much as Silver did. "Oh, Silver, I'm so sorry I didn't listen when you wanted to talk about how worried you were that Moonbeam had seen you vanish. I promise I'll always listen in the future. You're the most important thing in the world to me."

"More important than music?" asked Silver shyly.

"Even more important than that," said Aisha.

Silver snorted happily. "And I'm sorry that I worried you. Sometimes I don't think before I act.

In the future, I'll try to tell you what I'm planning before I do it."

Anxiously, Zara looked around. "Hey, guys, we need to move. Let's try to follow the glacier down—" She broke off as a low rumbling filled the air. As the noise grew louder, a familiar voice echoed across the glacier.

"You will never escape me! Never!"

The rumbling became a roar. Aisha stared in disbelief as the top of the mountain seemed to slide closer. Blinking, she realized a gigantic wall of snow was falling from the top, straight toward them.

"Avalanche!" she shrieked.

CHAPTER 9

There was no time to race for cover from the wall of snow thundering toward them, spewing rocks and boulders in all directions.

"What are we going to do?" shouted Phoebe.

"Feather!" cried Lily as a huge slab of rock crashed down a short distance away. "Can you lift the rock? We could hide under it!"

Feather stamped the ground with her hoof, and pink sparks flew up. The slab rose into the air and floated against the mountainside, forming a roof. Everyone rushed underneath it.

"You've got this," Lily said, stroking Feather's neck. "You can do it!"

The air seemed to shake as the wall of snow fell. It crashed down around them, and for a moment the noise was so loud, it hurt their ears. Aisha reached for Lily, placing a hand on her

arm as the snow thundered past them, slamming into the slab and pouring away. Feather's magic kept the slab in place. At last, the thundering stopped.

Feather floated the rock away from them and laid it down on the glacier. The girls looked around them. Snow was piled up against the base of the cliffs, and rocks were all over the glacier's snow-covered surface. Even the frozen saber-toothed polar bear had a thick covering of snow over its icy surface.

"Phew! That was close. Thanks for saving us, Feather," said Zara.

"Thanks, Feather," everyone else said.

"Let's get out of here!" said Aisha.

"Stop right there!" The count's voice snapped through the icy air as he came out of the cave beside the frozen bear. He held up his portable weather machine. "You're going nowhere."

"Really?" said Phoebe, her eyebrows arching. "Let me introduce you to my unicorn, Shimmer. The real Shimmer, whose mane is a different color at the moment but whose magic is just as powerful as you said. Shimmer, why don't you show him what you can do?"

Before the count could react, Shimmer struck the ground with his hoof and fired a bolt of energy magic into the fresh snow beside the count. The snow exploded. Shooting into the air, it fell down over the count, burying him completely.

He fought to get free from the snow. As his head and hands burst out, his fingers moved on the controls of his weather machine.

Feather quickly banged her hoof, and her magic plucked the weather machine from the count's grasp. It soared toward the girls, landing

in front of them. Zara grabbed it and pointed it at the count. "Let's see how you like being frozen!" she cried as she pushed down on the blue button.

"How dare you!" screamed the count. "How—" His voice cut off as a jet of water hit him and he froze, his mouth still open in fury.

The count's half-finished sentence echoed around the glacier. For a moment, no one spoke.

"We did it," Zara said, breaking the silence. "We saved Unicorn Island from the count."

Aisha bit her lip. "He . . . He isn't dead, is he?"

"No. When magic and science aren't combined, the effects can be reversed," said Zara. "Mr. Long taught us that in our tornado lesson. I guess you weren't listening." She grinned. "As usual."

Aisha made a face at her.

Lily looked relieved. "So the bear can be

defrosted too? I know it was attacking us, but it was only doing what bears do. And it doesn't seem fair to leave it frozen."

Zara examined the device in her hands. "There's probably a way we can do it using this, but I'm not sure which button to press."

"Wait," said Silver. "Aisha, do you still have that pink diamond you picked up earlier? You said it could melt anything."

Aisha drew the jewel from her pocket. "Yes, it's here. Let's try it out on the saber-toothed polar bear. But not Count Thornberry. Ms. Nettles can deal with him."

"Good idea," said Silver. "Feather, can you use your magic to touch the bear with the diamond?"

"Hang on!" said Phoebe. "You're all forgetting something. We're stuck here with no way home.

The last thing we want is an angry bear chasing us!"

Suddenly they heard a whistling sound above them and glanced up.

A man was falling out of the sky!

CHAPTER 10

"Watch out!" yelled Zara. They jumped back as the man landed with a plop in a pile of soft snow.

It was Mr. Long!

Sitting up, his fingers closed on something in his hand. "Girls, what are you doing here?" he said, shocked. He got to his feet, his eyes widening as he noticed the frozen count.

"I knew it!" gasped Zara. "Mr. Long is working with the count and he's come to rescue him!" Zara aimed the weather machine at him. "Well, stop right there, Mr. Long. You're toast—well, ice!"

"Wait!" Mr. Long held up his hands. "Please,

put that thing down, Zara. I can assure you I am not here to help the count."

Zara held the weather machine steady. "A likely story!"

"No, please listen!" begged Mr. Long.

Aisha stepped forward. "Zara, wait, we should hear Mr. Long's side before we zap him." She glanced at Silver. "It's really important to listen when others have something to say."

Silver nuzzled her.

Zara nodded slowly. "All right. We're listening, Mr. Long."

"Thank you," said Mr. Long. "I was grading the projects you did while you were in detention. Aisha wrote about Count Thornberry, mentioning that he had a secret lab in the ice caves of Diamond Glacier."

"Aisha!" Zara exclaimed. "We agreed not to write about the count."

Aisha blushed as all eyes turned to her. "Did we? I . . . um . . . might not have been listening."

The others groaned.

"Well, it's lucky you did," said Mr. Long. "I'd suspected that the count was behind the extreme weather disasters ever since I found a notebook he'd written. It was inside an abandoned cottage near where the tidal wave struck. I didn't have any proof that he was responsible, though, and I couldn't track him down. His family castle was boarded up, and I didn't know about the secret lab until I read Aisha's report. I told Ms. Nettles my suspicions, and she allowed me to ask the magic map to bring me to Diamond Glacier. I was prepared to face the count, but it looks like you've done my job already."

Zara slowly relaxed. "So you're not working with him."

"No," said Mr. Long. "He may be a great scientist, but he is arrogant, vain, and cruel. I love this fascinating island, and I promise you that I would never do anything to hurt it. As well as being an inspector, I am part of a group of scientists who want to protect the island. We've had suspicions about the count for some time. Now that we know he was behind the weather disasters, he must answer for the damage he's caused. Shall we go back to school, and then I can get the right people to deal with the count?"

"That sounds like a *very* good idea!" said Phoebe.

"But how do we get back?" said Zara.

Aisha's eyes sparkled. "Zara, weren't you listening?" she teased. "Mr. Long said he came here using the magic map. Which means that the thing he's holding in his hand . . ."

"Is the little model that will help us get back to the school!" finished Silver.

"It always appears when people use the map," said Aisha. "Or had you forgotten?"

Zara grinned at the teasing. "Okay. Maybe I prefer it when you don't listen, Aisha!"

Silver turned to nuzzle Aisha's black ponytail and gasped. He lifted up a streak of green, silver, and red with his muzzle. "We've bonded, Aisha! Look!"

Aisha squealed with joy. Putting her arms around Silver, she hugged him tightly while her friends cheered and their unicorns stamped their hooves. Even Mr. Long smiled. When they all finished congratulating Aisha and Silver, Mr. Long held out the little model of the academy. Clearing his throat, he said, "I believe we need to hold hands."

The girls swiftly grabbed hold of each other.

"You can probably just hold Moonbeam's mane," Zara said to Mr. Long.

He looked almost as relieved as the girls!

"Wait!" Aisha squeaked. "Before we go, Feather, can you use your moving magic to put this pink diamond on the bear?" She pulled the diamond out of her pocket.

"Of course." Feather sent the crystal flying from Aisha's hand and dropped it on the bear's head. Immediately the snow on the bear melted and the ice began to crack. The bear shook its head and started to roar.

"To Unicorn Academy!" cried Mr. Long quickly.

Aisha rose off the ground, and a moment later she felt herself spinning through the air. In no time at all, they arrived back at the academy, landing beside the enormous map in the hall.

Ms. Nettles was waiting beside it with Ms. Tulip and Ms. Rosemary. "You're back!" she exclaimed. "And, girls! What are you doing? Were you in the Wastelands?"

"We were kidnapped by Count Thornberry!" said Phoebe.

"Really?" Ms. Nettles exclaimed. "You had better come to my study and tell me exactly what has been going on!"

Between them, the girls and Mr. Long explained everything. Ms. Tulip barely waited for them to finish before she jumped to her feet. "My hero," she said, gazing at Mr. Long.

Mr. Long gave a modest cough. "The girls are the real heroes. They kept their wits about them when the count snatched them from the school grounds. They managed to escape, and they also stopped him from doing any more damage. I merely brought them home."

"What will happen to his weather machines?" asked Zara.

"Once Lysander is locked away, I shall return

to his lab and personally see that everything is destroyed," said Mr. Long. "No one is getting their hands on any of his equipment or notes. It would be too dangerous."

"Well," said Ms. Nettles. "I'm impressed, girls. Your bravery saved the island. You have also learned an important lesson." Her glasses rattled as she looked at each of the girls. "Never judge a person by first appearances. Mr. Long, thank you for the work you have done. If you're ever interested, I would be happy to offer you a job as a science teacher. I have had excellent reports about the science lesson you taught the other day from both the staff and students."

Mr. Long flushed. "Well . . . er . . . I have to say I did find teaching that lesson surprisingly enjoyable, Ms. Nettles. Maybe I will consider your offer."

Behind his back, Phoebe grimaced but Aisha

chuckled. Mr. Long wasn't that bad. Besides, in a month's time, they would be done with school and heading for lots of new adventures!

The day of graduation was bright and sunny with a crisp frost. Aisha was happy with the music and they'd practiced a lot, but her stomach still fizzed with nerves. The unicorns were brushed, their hooves painted with glitter, and their manes braided with ribbons.

The first parents arrived as lunch was finishing, and the dorms came out one by one to perform. Topaz dorm was before Amethyst.

"What if no one likes my music?" Aisha whispered to Silver as they watched the boys doing an acrobatic display on their unicorns' backs.

He nuzzled her. "Why wouldn't they? It's amazing."

Looking into his dark eyes, Aisha realized that as long as Silver liked her music, nothing else mattered.

As the first bars of her music floated into the arena, Aisha's worries melted away. The parents and teachers clapped in time to the beat. Feather used moving magic to hide various objects. Then Moonbeam located the objects using seer magic to help her predict where they were. Feather moved a pile of snow banked up outside the arena, building a giant snowman. While the parents watched, Silver turned invisible, and he and Aisha rode to the center to stand by the snowman's side. Feather stood back with a bow and Shimmer exploded the snowman with energy magic. As the flakes of snow floated to the ground, Silver and Aisha appeared as if by magic, and the audience applauded joyfully.

After the displays were over, everyone praised

Aisha for her music. The graduation ceremony followed. Aisha saw her parents clapping proudly in the audience as she went to get her scroll, and her heart swelled. After, the students and parents ate and danced in the hall, which had been decorated with stars, rainbows, and twinkling lights.

"We did it," Zara said when, finally, the girls and their unicorns went outside to watch the fireworks. "We're guardians now."

"I can barely believe it," said Lily.

"I'm going to miss everyone," said Phoebe, her eyes filling with tears.

"We'll still see each other," said Aisha.

"Soon," said Zara. "First sleepover is at my house!"

They hugged as the first fireworks exploded in the sky.

Silver rested his head against Aisha's shoulder

as the sky burst with colors. "I'm glad we found your magic and graduated with everyone else," Aisha whispered. "But I'm even happier that Ms. Nettles chose you to be my unicorn."

"Me too. We're going to have so many more adventures together. I just know it!"

Aisha turned and kissed his nose just as a huge red firework heart exploded in the air. Silver stamped his hoof, and he and Aisha vanished from sight. Facing each other in the middle of the crowd, they shared a special secret moment together as the heart fell from the sky in a stream of glittering red stars.

What if your best friend was a unicorn?

Sparkle Lake gives unicorns their magic,
but something is wrong with the water!
Can Sophia and Rainbow find out what's
going on before it's too late?

Don't miss where it all began!
Read on for a peek at the first book
in the Unicorn Academy series!

CHAPTER 1

"We're almost at the school!" exclaimed Sophia, seeing a sign just ahead. The swirly gold writing on it said UNICORN ACADEMY beside a painting of a snow-white unicorn with a rainbow arching over its head. An arrow pointed up a long, tree-lined drive.

"Race you!" called Harry, Sophia's seven-year-old brother.

Sophia couldn't wait to see the school after five hours of riding, and she would have loved to gallop, but she slid from her shaggy gray pony's back and patted his neck fondly. "Sorry, Harry, but Clover's tired. I'm not going to make him race."

Clover, who was old and couldn't go fast anymore, pushed his nose gratefully into Sophia's hair. Her wavy black curls hung over his muzzle like a droopy mustache. Sophia giggled, but there was a heavy weight in her stomach. Now that she was ten, she was thrilled to be old enough to attend Unicorn Academy and finally get a unicorn of her own. But she was really going to miss Clover!

"All right, sweetie?" asked her mom, trotting up alongside. Solitaire, her mom's unicorn, was fully grown and looked very elegant compared to short-legged Clover. "You're going to have a fantastic time here at the school, but I expect it feels quite strange at the moment. Remember to be polite and please try to think first before rushing into things."

Sophia grinned. "As if I'd do that, Mom!"

"Hmm," her mom said, raising her eyebrows.

Then her expression softened. "Remember that all the other girls and boys will probably be feeling as nervous as you. But it won't be long before you get to know each other."

"I am a little bit nervous about making friends," admitted Sophia, "but I'm more worried about Clover." She stroked Clover's neck. "Do you think he'll be okay without me?"

"He'll be fine," said her mom. "He's getting old, and he'll be happy having a quieter life. Harry and I will make sure he gets lots of cuddles. Don't worry about Clover. Just enjoy getting to know your own special unicorn, bonding and learning to work together to protect our island."

Sophia's heart swelled. She loved the thought of protecting Unicorn Island, their beautiful home. "I wonder what my unicorn will be like and what its magical power will be. I hope it can heal like Solitaire."

Each unicorn was born with its own special magical power. There were many different powers, and young unicorns usually found out what they could do in their first year at Unicorn Academy.

Sophia's mom leaned down to push a stray black curl out of Sophia's eyes. "I'm sure you'll love your unicorn, whatever power it has."

Sophia fell quiet as she climbed back onto Clover and rode him through the green tunnel of trees toward the school. She really wanted her unicorn to be able to heal. With healing magic, maybe she could take away some of Clover's aches and pains.

The tunnel ended, and Sophia rode Clover out into the pale January sunlight.

MerMiCORns

Swim into a new series!

MerMiCORns ①

Sparkle Magic

Sudipta Bardhan-Quallen

Mermicorns are part unicorn, part mermaid, and totally magical!

rhcbooks.com RHCB

PuRRmaiDs
Meet your newest feline friends!
1
PuRRmaiDs
The Scaredy Cat
Sudipta Bardhan-Quallen
Cover art copyright © 2019 by Andrew Farley. Purrmaids® is a registered trademark of KIKIDOODLE LLC and is used under license from KIKIDOODLE LLC.
1277a
rhcbooks.com
RHCB

Collect all the books in the
Horse Diaries series!

Elska

CATHERINE HAPKA
illustrated by RUTH SANDERSON

Bell's Star

ALISON HART
illustrated by RUTH SANDERSON

Koda

PATRICIA HERMES
illustrated by RUTH SANDERSON

Luna

CATHERINE HAPKA
illustrated by RUTH SANDERSON

Cinders

KATE KLIMO
illustrated by RUTH SANDERSON

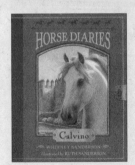

Calvino

WHITNEY SANDERSON
illustrated by RUTH SANDERSON

New friends. New adventures.
Find a new series . . . just for you!

ISADORA MOON

For ballerina and fairy and vampire lovers

MAGIC ON THE MAP

For adventurers

UNICORN ACADEMY

For unicorn lovers

PUPPY PIRATES

For dog lovers

PuRRmaids

For mermaid and cat lovers

BALLPARK Mysteries

For sports fans

Isadora Moon: cover art © Harriet Muncaster. Magic on the Map: cover art © Stevie Lewis. Unicorn Academy: cover art © Lucy Truman. Puppy Pirates: cover art © Luz Tapia.
Purrmaids: cover art © Andrew Farley. Purrmaids® is a registered trademark of KINDOODLE LLC and is used under license from KINDOODLE LLC. Ballpark Mysteries: cover art © Mark Meyers.

RHCB rhcbooks.com